this book belongs to

Sara

children's choice®

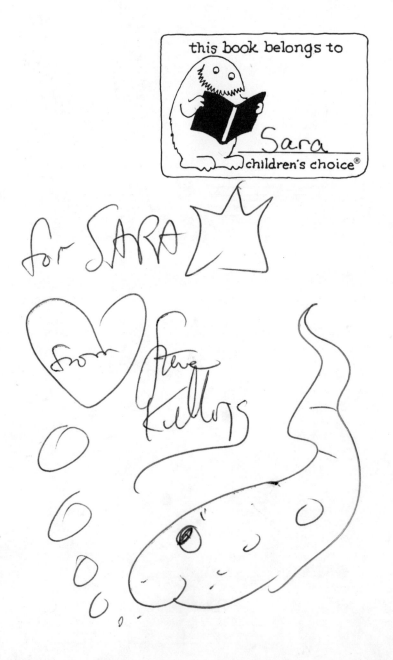

for SARA

from *Steve Kellogg*

THE
MYSTERIOUS
TADPOLE

STEVEN KELLOGG

THE DIAL PRESS · NEW YORK

A Children's Choice® Book Club Edition From Scholastic Book Services

Printed in the United States of America

ISBN 0-590-75939-6

For Joseph

Uncle McAllister lived in Scotland. Every year he sent Louis a birthday gift for his nature collection.

"This is the best one yet!" cried Louis.

The next day he took his entire collection to school for show-and-tell.

"Class, this is a tadpole," said Mrs. Shelbert. She asked Louis to bring it back often so they could all watch it become a frog.

Louis named the tadpole Alphonse. Every day Alphonse
ate several cheeseburgers.

Louis found that he was eager to learn.

When Alphonse became too big for his jar, Louis moved
him to the sink.

After Alphonse outgrew the sink, Louis's parents agreed to let him use the bathtub.

One day Mrs. Shelbert decided that Alphonse was not turning into an ordinary frog.

She asked Louis to stop bringing him to school.

By the time summer vacation arrived, Alphonse was enormous.

"He's too big for the bathtub," said Louis's mother.

"He's too big for the apartment," said Louis's father.

"He needs a swimming pool," said Louis.

"There is no place in our apartment for a swimming pool," said his parents.

Louis suggested that they buy the parking lot next door and build a swimming pool.

"It would cost more money than we have," said his parents. "Your tadpole will have to be donated to the zoo."

The thought of Alphonse in a cage made Louis very sad.

Then, in the middle of the night, Louis remembered that the junior high had a swimming pool that nobody used during the summer.

Louis hid Alphonse under a rug and smuggled him into the school.

After making sure that Alphonse felt at home, Louis went back to bed.

Every morning Louis spent several hours swimming with his friend. In the afternoon he earned the money for Alphonse's cheeseburgers by delivering newspapers.

Meanwhile the training continued. Alphonse learned to retrieve things from the bottom of the pool.

Summer vacation passed quickly. Louis worried what would happen to Alphonse now that school had reopened.

As soon as the first day ended, he ran to the junior high. The students were getting ready for after-school activities.

Louis arrived just as the first swimming race began.

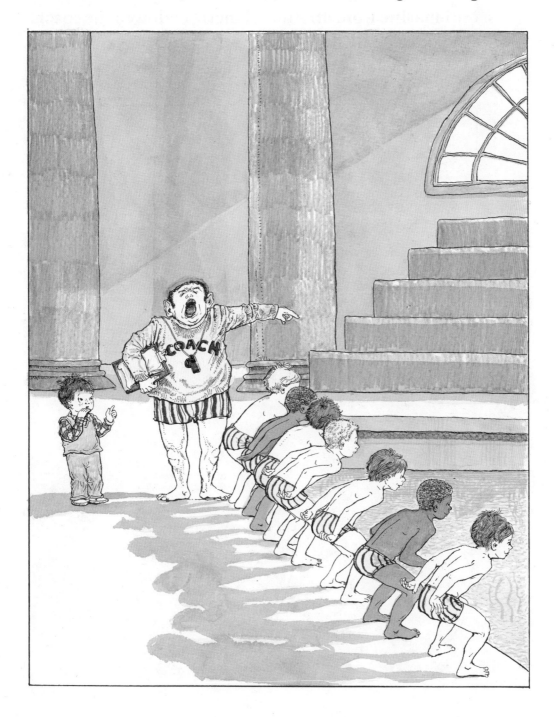

Alphonse was delighted to see all the swimmers.

"It's a submarine from another planet!" bellowed the coach. "Call the police! Call the Navy!"

"No! It's a tadpole!" cried Louis. "He's my pet!"

The coach was upset and confused.

"You have until tomorrow," he cried, "to get that creature out of the pool!"

Louis didn't know what to do. On the way home he met his friend Miss Seevers, the librarian, and he told her his problem.

Miss Seevers went back to the junior high school with Louis, but when she saw Alphonse, she was so shocked that she dropped her purse and the books she was carrying into the swimming pool. Alphonse retrieved them.

Then Miss Seevers telephoned Louis's Uncle McAllister in Scotland. He told her that he had caught the little tadpole in Loch Ness, a large lake near his cottage.

Miss Seevers said, "I'm convinced that your uncle has given you a very rare Loch Ness monster!"

"I don't care!" cried Louis. "He's my pet, and I love him!" He begged Miss Seevers to help him raise enough money to buy the parking lot near his apartment so he could build a swimming pool for Alphonse.

Suddenly Miss Seevers had an idea.

"In 1639 there was a battle in our city's harbor," she said. "A pirate treasure ship was sunk, and no one has ever been able to find it. But perhaps we can!"

The next morning Miss Seevers and Louis rented a boat.

In the middle of the harbor Louis showed Alphonse a picture of a treasure chest.

Alphonse disappeared under the water.

Louis and Miss Seevers bought the parking lot.

They hired some helpers.

And when the pool was completed,

all the children in the city were invited to swim.

That night Louis said, "Alphonse, next week is my birthday, which means that we've been friends for almost a year."

Far away in Scotland Uncle McAllister was also thinking
about the approaching birthday. While out hiking he dis-
covered an unusual stone in a clump of grass and sticks.
"A perfect gift for my nephew!" he cried.
"I'll deliver it in person!"

Uncle McAllister arrived at Louis's apartment and gave Louis the present.

Louis couldn't wait to add it to his collection.

Suddenly a crack appeared in the stone....

The Children's Choice® Clubhouse

It's the perfect place for playing or for curling up with a good book ★ Big enough to hold a few friends (it's 3′ x 4½′ and 4½′ tall) ★ Made of sturdy corrugated cardboard with a washable finish ★ Decorated inside and out with whimsical illustrations in full color ★ A very special gift.

To order, please send your name and address with a check or money order for $19.95 to:

**Children's Choice® Clubhouse
Scholastic Inc.
900 Sylvan Ave.
Englewood Cliffs
New Jersey 07632**